RAINBOW magic®

The Music Fairies

Special thanks to
Narinder Dhami

ORCHARD BOOKS
338 Euston Road, London NW1 3BH
Orchard Books Australia
Level 17/207 Kent Street, Sydney, NSW 2000
A Paperback Original

First published in 2008 by Orchard Books.

HiT entertainment

A CIP catalogue record for this book is available
from the British Library.

ISBN 978 1 40830 029 9
3 5 7 9 10 8 6 4 2

Printed and bound in China by Imago

Orchard Books is a division of Hachette Children's Books,
an Hachette UK company

www.hachette.co.uk

Fiona the Flute Fairy

by Daisy Meadows

ORCHARD BOOKS

www.rainbowmagic.co.uk

I'm through with frost, ice and snow.
To the human world I must go!
I'll form a cool, Gobolicious Band.
Magical instruments will lend a hand.

With these instruments I'll go far.
Frosty Jack, a superstar.
I'll steal music's harmony and fun.
Watch out world, I'll be number one!

Contents

Card Trick

"Oh, this is one of my favourite shops in Wetherbury!" Rachel Walker stopped outside Sparkly Wishes and turned to her best friend, Kirsty Tate. "They always have such gorgeous cards and gifts. Can we go in?"

"OK," Kirsty agreed, pushing open the shop door. "Do you want to buy something or just look around?"

9

"I want to get a thank you card to give to your parents when I go home at the end of half term," Rachel replied, as they went inside.

Kirsty smiled. "Oh, that's lovely, Rachel!"

"I'll get a card to send to Mum and Dad, too," Rachel went on, "just to say that I'm fine, and having a great time." She grinned. "Although Mum and Dad know that I *always* have a great time when I stay with you, Kirsty."

"They don't know that we're friends with the fairies and have lots of

exciting, magical adventures, though!"
Kirsty pointed out.

Rachel nodded. The Music
Fairies had asked for
the girls' help after
Jack Frost and his
naughty goblin
servants had
stolen the seven
Magical Musical
Instruments from the
Fairyland School of Music.
These special instruments made
music fun and harmonious in
both the human and fairy worlds,
and without them, music everywhere
sounded terrible and out of tune.

Rachel and Kirsty had been horrified
to discover that Jack Frost intended to

use the instruments' magical powers to win the National Talent Competition that was taking place at the New Harmony Mall near Wetherbury.

Jack Frost was determined to win the first prize of a recording contract with MegaBig Records, and had sent his goblins to hide out in Wetherbury with the Magical Musical Instruments, ready for the competition at the weekend. But, with the help of the Music Fairies, the girls were determined to foil his plans and return all the instruments to Fairyland before Rachel went home at the end of half term.

"I hope we find another Magical Musical Instrument today," Rachel said, as she flipped through a rack of glittery cards. "We've managed to return

Poppy's piano and Ellie's guitar, but we need to find all the other instruments, so music isn't ruined forever!"

"I know," Kirsty agreed. "But

remember what Queen Titania always says? We have to let the magic come to *us*."

"It's hard though, isn't it?" Rachel sighed.

"*Really* hard!" Kirsty agreed.

She left Rachel to choose her cards and went over to look at a display of cute teddy bears. There weren't any other customers in the shop, except for a little boy and his mother, and Kirsty wandered around, looking at whatever caught her eye.

Suddenly she spotted a large, brightly coloured card at the front of a nearby

display. The card was covered with silver sparkles and in the middle was a pretty little fairy with long red hair. *She looks a bit like Poppy the Piano Fairy!* Kirsty thought, smiling to herself.

Kirsty took the card to show Rachel, who was looking at postcards of views of Wetherbury.

"Does this remind you of anyone, Rachel?" asked Kirsty, holding the card out.

"Oh, yes – Poppy!" Rachel exclaimed. "Maybe I should send that card to my mum and dad. What does it say inside, Kirsty?"

Kirsty flipped the card open. Immediately a puff of glitter burst out, showering both girls with sparkles. Rachel and Kirsty gasped as a tiny fairy popped out of the card and waved at them. She wore a metallic silver dress with Roman-style sandals, and her dark hair was braided with beads.

"Hi, girls," she called. "I'm Fiona the Flute Fairy!"

"We're so glad to see you, Fiona," Rachel said eagerly.

"Do you think your Magic Flute is nearby?" asked Kirsty.

Fiona nodded solemnly. "And I hope you'll help me find it, girls," she went on. "There's no time to waste! Did you know that Jack Frost and his goblins are going to enter the National Talent Competition next weekend?"

"Oh, yes." Rachel grinned. "We've heard all about Frosty and his Gobolicious Band!" Fiona smiled.

"We've heard rumours in Fairyland that Jack Frost is writing his own songs for the competition," she told them.  "So far his works include *You've Got To Be Cold To Be Kind*, *Green With Envy* and *Fairyland Rock!*"

The girls laughed.

"I wonder what his songs are like?" said Rachel.

"Even if they're *awful*," Fiona replied, "Jack Frost will still win the talent competition with the help of the Magical Musical Instruments!"

"Then he'll get the recording contract with MegaBig Records," Kirsty pointed out. "If he becomes a famous pop star, everyone will want to know all about him."

"And that would mean disaster for Fairyland!" Fiona sighed, her wings drooping a little. "You know that we can't let *anyone* find out about the existence of fairies. Girls, we *have* to stop Jack Frost!"

"Well, let's start by looking for your flute," Kirsty said in a determined voice.

"It's not far away, I know it!" Fiona replied, fluttering down to sit on Kirsty's shoulder.

"I can feel its beautiful music calling to me."

Rachel was about to say something when a movement outside the shop window caught her eye. Suddenly, to her surprise, a group of people went dancing past the Sparkly Wishes card shop!

Follow the Music!

Amazed, Rachel rubbed her eyes.
Was she seeing things?

Curiously, she peered outside.
The dancers were moving down
the High Street. There was a painter
still holding his wet brush, which
left a trail of green paint behind
him as he twirled round a lamp post.

A mother with a pram was skipping along, her baby chuckling with delight, and a man in a suit was waltzing and talking into his mobile phone at the same time.

"Kirsty!" Rachel tugged her friend's sleeve. "You *have* to see this!"

Kirsty looked up. "What's happening?" she asked, puzzled.

At that moment the little boy, who was looking at the display of teddies, glanced outside and spotted the dancers.

"Look, Mum, it's a parade!" he yelled excitedly.

"Let's go and watch," his mum replied, and they hurried out of the card shop, leaving the door open behind them. Immediately, the sound of sweet, melodic music drifted in from the street.

"What beautiful music!" Rachel said dreamily. "What's the parade for, Kirsty?"

"I don't know," Kirsty replied,
swaying in time to the music. "I had
no idea there was going to be a parade
in Wetherbury today."

"Girls, listen to me!" Fiona said
anxiously. But Rachel and Kirsty didn't
even look at her.

"I *have* to find out where this amazing
music is coming from!" Rachel went on,
heading for the door.

"I know it's strange, but there's just *something* about this music," Kirsty agreed. "I *must* follow it!" And she rushed after Rachel.

"That's just it, girls!" Fiona darted in front of them, blocking their path. "This wonderful music is coming from my Magic Flute!"

Rachel and Kirsty stared at her.

"People can't resist the sweet sounds of my flute, and that means it could be dangerous in the wrong hands," Fiona explained quickly.

She waved her wand to break the spell the flute had cast over the girls.

"We must get it back, then," said Rachel, giving herself a little shake. Fiona swooped into Rachel's pocket and the three friends rushed outside.

The High Street was now crowded with people dancing around.

Even the cars had stopped and their drivers had got out to join in.

"The music's getting fainter." Fiona looked worried. "That means whoever has my flute is moving away. I'll turn you both into fairies, so we can fly after them."

Rachel and Kirsty hurried into a nearby phone box.

Fiona flew out of Rachel's pocket
and quickly showered both girls
with a cloud of
shimmering sparkles.
Instantly the two
girls shrank down
to fairy-size, with
translucent wings
on their shoulders.

"Let's go!" Fiona
cried, soaring out
of the phone box.

Rachel and Kirsty
followed, and the three
of them zoomed along the
High Street, keeping high
above the heads of the dancing
crowds and following the faint,
sweet melody of the flute.

"We must be on the look-out for goblins," Kirsty said. "Remember that Jack Frost's spell has made them look more like humans."

"Yes, they're boy-sized and human-coloured," Rachel agreed as they wove their way between the street lights. "But the spell didn't work completely, so we can recognise them from their big noses, ears and feet!"

"The music's getting louder again," Fiona said, looking around. Suddenly she gave a gasp of delight. "There's my flute!"

Rachel and Kirsty saw a little girl in a pink party dress and matching hat. She was skipping along, playing the Magic Flute. The beautiful tune brought people out of the shops and into the street, to join the dancing as the little girl passed by.

"After her!" Rachel cried, but Kirsty caught her arm.

"Wait!" she said. "Who are *they*?" And she pointed down at two strange-looking boys chasing after the little girl.

Their large noses and ears were poking out from under their baseball caps, and their trainers looked very big indeed. They were arguing bitterly as they raced towards the girl, although the three friends couldn't hear what they were saying.

"Goblins!" Rachel gasped.

"We must stop them stealing my flute from the little girl!" Fiona exclaimed.

Fiona, Rachel and Kirsty hovered above the girl, and then ducked down to hide behind one of the white daisies on her pink hat. Then Rachel peeped cautiously over the brim at the little girl's face.

"Look at that big nose and those pointy ears!" Rachel whispered. "That's no little girl with the Magic Flute — that's a goblin!"

Tug of War!

Fiona and Kirsty bent forward to look but Fiona's gossamer wings tickled the goblin's ear. Irritably, he swatted her away and she tumbled out of the hat.

"Fiona, are you OK?" Rachel asked anxiously, as she and Kirsty rushed out from behind the daisy.

"I'm fine!" Fiona panted, pausing in mid air to give her crumpled wings a shake.

"Look out! Fairy alert!" roared a gruff voice.

Dismayed, Fiona, Rachel and Kirsty looked round. The boy goblins were rushing towards them, yelling loudly.

Fiona grabbed Kirsty's and Rachel's hands and pulled them towards a nearby tree, where they hid among the autumn leaves.

The "girl" goblin lowered the flute and glared at the other two.

"Stop shouting!" he grumbled. "You're interrupting my beautiful music!"

"But we saw *fairies*—" the biggest of the boy goblins began.

"Nonsense!" snapped the "girl" goblin, glancing around. Because the music had stopped, people had stopped dancing too, and the crowd was beginning to break up.

"There are no fairies here!" He eyed the other two goblins suspiciously. "I thought my disguise might fool you, but I know what you're up to," he went on. "You just want to steal my Magic Flute!"

"Well, now that you mention it..." said the smallest goblin cheekily. And he lunged forward, and grabbed one end of the flute. "Let us have a go!"

"Shan't!" yelled the other goblin, holding onto the mouthpiece of the flute for dear life.

The girls watched in horror as the two goblins began playing tug of war with Fiona's flute.

"The flute's breaking!" Kirsty exclaimed.

"Don't worry," Fiona explained quickly. "Flutes are *meant* to come apart in three pieces!"

As the goblins pulled harder, the flute broke into sections. The two goblins were left with a piece each, and the middle section clattered to the ground. The other goblin snatched it up immediately.

"Now we've *all* got a flute!" he boasted. He put the piece to his lips, and the goblin with the end piece did the same. But when they blew into them, nothing happened.

"You idiots!" the "girl" goblin sniggered, holding up the mouthpiece. "You can't play a flute without *this*!"

The other two goblins made a grab for him. But he dodged them and dashed off, still laughing. Scowling, the others raced after him.

Rachel, Kirsty and Fiona zoomed after the goblins. But they found it difficult to stay with them because they had to keep ducking and diving to make sure they weren't spotted by any of the shoppers.

"We mustn't lose them!" Rachel panted as the goblins raced past the Wetherbury Museum.

"They're going towards Willow Hill!" Kirsty cried as, suddenly, the goblins veered sharply away from the High Street and headed out into the surrounding countryside.

"Perfect!" Fiona replied. "We'll be able to fly more quickly once we're out of the village and don't have to worry about being seen."

The goblins had all kicked off their shoes so that they could run even faster, although the "girl" goblin was still wearing his dress, wig and hat. Now they rushed into the woods on Willow Hill. Fiona, Rachel and Kirsty flew through the trees after them, speeding up now that it was safe to do so. It didn't take them long to reach the goblins.

"Give me back my flute!" Fiona demanded.

The goblins almost jumped out of their skins.

"Fairies!" they screeched, and immediately took off in three different directions.

"Which way shall we go?" Kirsty cried.

"We'll take one at a time," Fiona decided quickly. "That one first!" And she pointed at the goblin who had the end section of the flute.

The goblin was weaving his way in and out of the trees, the end piece clutched firmly in his hand. Fiona, Rachel and Kirsty raced after him.

"Why don't you just give up?" Rachel yelled. "You're no match for us all!"

The goblin chuckled. "Actually," he said smugly, twisting round to look at Rachel, "three silly fairies are no match for *me!*"

The goblin was so intent on boasting and bragging that he didn't look where he was going. There was a log in his path and he tripped right over it, going head-over-heels with a loud shriek.

As he fell, the goblin lost his grip on the flute piece. It flew from his hand and sailed through the air!

41

Double Trouble

"Quick!" Fiona cried.

She and the girls rushed towards the section of flute as it tumbled downwards. Between the three of them they managed to catch it before it hit the ground. Then, with a whisk of Fiona's wand, a puff of glittering magic dust shrank the piece back to its Fairyland size.

"We'd better see if the goblin is OK," said Rachel.

The goblin had luckily made a soft landing in a pile of autumn leaves. As Rachel hovered above the pile, the goblin emerged from it, dusting himself down and muttering crossly. But Rachel thought she was seeing things when a *second* goblin also popped his head out of the leaves!

"Look," she called to Kirsty and Fiona. "The goblins are multiplying!"

"This silly goblin landed right in the middle of my hiding-place!" shouted the second goblin furiously.

"You shut up!" screeched the first goblin, and the two of them began to wrestle, sending the leaves spinning in all directions.

"Just give us the second piece of the flute!" said Kirsty.

The goblins stopped wrestling and stared down at their hands in panic.

"I haven't *got* my piece!" groaned the first goblin.

"Nor me!" added the second. "You stole it!"

"No, I didn't!" the first goblin declared.

As the goblins began arguing again, Rachel suddenly spotted a gleam of silver among the leaves. "Fiona, I think the missing piece is down there with the goblins!" she whispered. "But we need to move the leaves to get it."

Fiona pointed her
wand at the leaves
and began to sing:
*"Autumn leaves,
orange and gold,
Lie fallen on
the ground.
When you hear
my magical song,
Rise up and
dance around!"*
Immediately the
leaves rose up in
a huge cloud and
began to swirl
around the
two goblins.

"Help!" the first goblin yelled. He batted the leaves away and accidentally smacked the second goblin on the nose.

"Ow!" the second goblin roared, jumping up and down in a rage.

"There's the second piece of flute!" Rachel whispered.

The middle section of the flute now lay uncovered on the grass. Immediately, Fiona, Rachel and Kirsty swooped down, and a wave of

Fiona's wand transformed it back
to its Fairyland size. The
goblins were still trying to
fight their way out of
the cloud of leaves, so
Fiona and the girls
quickly flew away.
"Two down,
one to go!" Fiona
smiled as she fitted
the pieces together.
"Now, where's that
third goblin with the
mouthpiece?"
"He can't be far
away," Kirsty replied.
But the goblin seemed
to have disappeared. Fiona
and the girls hunted high and low,

behind trees and under bushes, but the goblin was nowhere to be found.

"What now?" asked Kirsty.

Fiona glanced up into one of the trees, where a squirrel sat, gnawing on a nut.

"Maybe we need some help," she replied.

Puzzled, Kirsty and Rachel watched as Fiona pursed her lips and whistled a short, magical tune.

"Now ask the squirrel if he's seen the goblin," Fiona said.

Rachel cleared her throat.

"Excuse me," she called. "We're looking for a goblin. Have you seen him?"

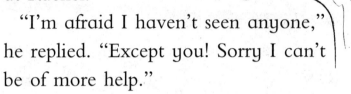

The squirrel
stopped gnawing
and looked down
at Rachel.

"I'm afraid I haven't seen anyone,"
he replied. "Except you! Sorry I can't
be of more help."

"I haven't seen any goblins either!"
chirped a bluebird that was nesting
higher up the tree.

"Thank you," Rachel
said with a smile.

Kirsty heard a
rustling noise and
spotted two rabbits in
the bushes.

"Can you help us,
please?" she asked. "We're looking for
a goblin."

"Oh, we haven't seen anyone," the rabbits replied politely, before hopping off across the grass. "Sorry!"

"Let's try a different part of the wood," Fiona said.

As they flew deeper among the trees, Rachel's eye was caught by a flash of russet-red in the undergrowth. A fox was sitting by a large bush.

"Let's ask that fox if he's seen the goblin," Rachel suggested. But as they swooped down, they could see that the fox looked very upset.

"Hello there," Fiona called. "What's the matter?"

The fox heaved a sigh. "Someone's stolen my den," he explained. "I built myself a cosy home among the roots of a big oak tree. But I popped out, just for a moment, and now someone's stolen it!"

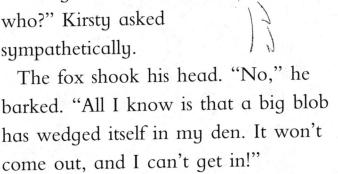

"Do you know who?" Kirsty asked sympathetically.

The fox shook his head. "No," he barked. "All I know is that a big blob has wedged itself in my den. It won't come out, and I can't get in!"

Fiona and the girls glanced at each other.

"Does this blob have a big nose?" asked Kirsty.

"And pointy ears?" said Rachel.

"And big feet?" Fiona added.

"Yes," the fox said. "And it's got a shiny stick."

"It's the goblin!" Rachel laughed.

Goblin in a Hole

"Can you take us to your home?"
Fiona asked the fox. "We might be
able to get it back for you!"

The fox nodded eagerly and trotted
off across the clearing. He led Fiona
and the girls over to a large, sturdy oak
tree and pointed his paw at a hole
under its trunk.

"Look!" the fox said. Rachel, Kirsty
and Fiona couldn't help laughing.
There, sticking out of
the entrance to the
fox's den, were two
large, dirty goblin
feet!

"Does the den
have a back
door?" asked Kirsty.

The fox trotted round the side of the
tree and showed Fiona and the girls
another hole.

"Wait here," said Fiona to the fox,
and she, Rachel and Kirsty flew inside.

The goblin was hunched inside the
fox's den, groaning to himself. The hole
was much too small for him and he
looked very cramped and uncomfortable.

"What are you pesky fairies doing here?" he demanded with a scowl.

"We've come to ask you to leave the fox's den, please!" said Fiona.

"It isn't nice to go into someone's house uninvited," added Rachel.

"I would if I could, but I can't!" the goblin replied. "I came in here to hide from *you*, but now I'm stuck and my pretty dress is ruined!"

"We'll help you get out if you give us your piece of the flute," Kirsty offered, trying not to laugh.

The goblin frowned. "But it plays such pretty music!" he said. Suddenly he began to squirm around and giggle. "That fox is nipping at my feet again," he chuckled. "It tickles. Make him stop!"

"Only if you give us the mouthpiece," Rachel said firmly.

"Hee hee!" the goblin laughed, wriggling around. "All right, then."

With a little effort he managed to lift his arm and pass the mouthpiece to Fiona.

"Thank you!" said Fiona. "Now we'll try to get you out."

The three friends flew out of the hole again. With a sprinkle of fairy dust, the mouthpiece shrank immediately and Fiona attached it to the rest of her flute.

"As good as new!" she said, giving it a kiss.

"Could you stop nipping at the goblin's feet?" Kirsty asked the fox. "If he stops wriggling about, maybe we can get him out of your den."

"I'm sure we can," Fiona added. "Girls, if I make you human-sized again, you can pull him out by his feet!"

Rachel and Kirsty nodded. With one wave of Fiona's wand, they instantly zoomed back up to their normal size.

Just as the girls were about to take hold of the goblin's feet, the other two goblins suddenly wandered into the clearing. They burst out laughing when they saw the goblin's feet sticking out of the fox's hole.

"What's he up to?" the biggest goblin sniggered.

"He's stuck and we're just about to pull him out," Kirsty explained.

The goblins laughed even louder.

"Here goes!" Rachel said, grasping one of the goblin's feet. "Oh, what is that horrible smell?"

"It's the goblin's stinky feet!" Kirsty groaned, holding her nose with one hand as she pulled on his other foot.

"I heard that!" the goblin in the hole shouted angrily.

The girls pulled as hard as they could but the goblin didn't budge. The other goblins thought this was hilarious. They danced around the tree singing:

"Goblin in a hole
and he can't get out,
Jack Frost's going to
scream and shout!"

Fiona lifted her flute to her lips.
"I think it's time for some Music Fairy
Magic!" she exclaimed.

Magical Melody

Fiona began to play her flute. As the
sweet, soothing notes drifted around
the clearing, some of the woodland
animals popped out of their homes
to listen. Even the goblins fell silent.

Suddenly Kirsty noticed that the oak tree was shaking and shuddering. She nudged Rachel.

"Look at the tree!" she whispered.

"It's *dancing*!" Rachel gasped, her eyes wide.

The tree was swaying its branches in time to the music. As it did so, it rose up a few centimetres, almost as if it were standing on tiptoe.

"Pull, Rachel!" Kirsty cried, grasping the goblin's foot tightly.

Now that the tree had risen up a little, the fox's den had become slightly bigger. Both girls tugged firmly on the goblin's feet, and suddenly he shot out of the hole like a cork from a bottle.

Fiona stopped playing and the tree sank down again. Meanwhile, the goblin climbed to his feet and scowled at his friends.

"I heard you laughing at me!" he snapped.

"Where's your piece of the flute?" the big goblin demanded.

"I had to give it to those pesky fairies to get me out of the hole!" the other goblin muttered.

"You idiot!" the two goblins yelled.

"Where are *your* pieces then?" the first goblin demanded, brushing down his dress.

The other two looked sheepish.

"*She's* got them!" they chorused, pointing at Fiona.

"So who's the idiot *now*?" the goblin in the dress jeered.

And, squabbling, the three goblins stomped off.

"Thank you for your help," the fox said happily, settling himself in the doorway of his den.

Fiona smiled and played another short burst of magical melody on her flute.

"My music will make sure you and your family will always be happy in your den," she explained.

Then she turned to Rachel and Kirsty. "Girls, thanks to you we have another of our precious Magical Musical Instruments back where it belongs!"

she said happily. "I must take my flute to Fairyland, but I know you'll do your very best to find the other instruments, so that we can stop Jack Frost from winning the talent competition!"

"We will!" Rachel and Kirsty cried as, in a dazzle of glitter, Fiona vanished, leaving a faint, sweet melody behind her.

Whistling Fiona's tune, Rachel and Kirsty hurried back to the High Street.

"Everything's back to normal," Rachel said, watching people going in and out of the shops.

"Yes, but imagine how much chaos there'll be if Frosty and his Gobolicious Band win the talent competition!" Kirsty pointed out. "Even if he only has *one* of the Magical Musical Instruments, Jack Frost will still win."

"Then we've just *got* to find the other four instruments before the weekend," Rachel said solemnly. "And then we can make sure that music is fun and harmonious again for *everyone!*"

Rachel and Kirsty must now help

Danni the Drum Fairy

The naughty goblins have Danni's
Magic Drums, and she needs Rachel's
and Kirsty's help to get them back!

Here's an extract from
Danni the Drum Fairy...

Extra-Exciting

"Bye, girls, I'll see you later," said Mrs Tate. "Have fun!"

"We will," Kirsty Tate replied, smiling. She leaned through the car window to kiss her mum goodbye. "Thanks for the lift. Bye!"

"Goodbye!" echoed Rachel Walker, Kirsty's best friend.

Both girls waved as Mrs Tate drove away. Kirsty looked up at the warehouse building they were standing in front of, and grinned at Rachel. "What are we waiting for?" she said. "Let's get inside!"

Rachel's eyes were bright as she slipped an arm through Kirsty's. "I can't believe we're actually going to be in a pop video!" she said happily. "As if this holiday wasn't already brilliant enough!"

The two girls walked through tall glass double doors into the warehouse, feeling bubbly with anticipation. Rachel was staying with Kirsty's family for a week over the half-term holiday, and on the very first day the girls had found themselves in another of their wonderful fairy adventures. This time they had been helping the Music Fairies find their Magical Musical Instruments which had been stolen by naughty Jack Frost and his goblins.

So far, the girls had helped the Music

Fairies find three of the instruments, but there were still four left to find.

Today, Kirsty and Rachel were in for a very different kind of adventure, though. Kirsty felt dizzy with excitement as she thought about it again. She and Rachel were so lucky to be here. They were both big fans of Juanita, the pop star who'd shot to fame last year when she'd won the National Talent Competition. And now Juanita was making a video for her new song right here in Wetherbury! Not only that, but Mrs Tate's friend, Mandy, had been hired as the make-up artist for the video shoot…and she'd asked if Kirsty and Rachel would like to appear in the video as extras! Both girls were so excited and had been practising the routine at home as much as possible.

Kirsty's and Rachel's legs were trembling as they walked into the warehouse. They found themselves in a smart lobby area, with a reception desk plus a couple of bright red sofas. VIDEO SHOOT THIS WAY read a sign on the far wall, with an arrow pointing along a corridor...

The Music Fairies

Win Rainbow Magic goodies!

In every book in the Rainbow Magic Music Fairies series
(books 64-70) there is a hidden picture of a musical note with a
secret letter in it. Find all seven letters and re-arrange them to make
a special Music Fairies word, then send it to us. Each month we will
put the entries into a draw and select one winner to receive
a Rainbow Magic Sparkly T-shirt and Goody Bag!

Send your entry on a postcard to Rainbow Magic Music Fairies
Competition, Orchard Books, 338 Euston Road, London NW1 3BH.
Australian readers should write to Hachette Children's Books,
Level 17/207 Kent Street, Sydney, NSW 2000.
New Zealand readers should write to Rainbow Magic Competition,
4 Whetu Place, Mairangi Bay, Auckland, NZ. Don't forget to
include your name and address. Only one entry per child.
Final draw: 30th September 2009.

Good luck!

Have you checked out the

website at:
www.rainbowmagic.co.uk

Look out for the
Magical Animal Fairies!

ASHLEY
THE DRAGON FAIRY
978-1-40830-349-8

LARA
THE BLACK CAT FAIRY
978-1-40830-350-4

ERIN
THE FIREBIRD FAIRY
978-1-40830-351-1

RIHANNA
THE SEAHORSE FAIRY
978-1-40830-352-8

SOPHIA
THE SNOW SWAN FAIRY
978-1-40830-353-5

LEONA
THE UNICORN FAIRY
978-1-40830-354-2

CAITLIN
THE ICE BEAR FAIRY
978-1-40830-355-9

Available
April 2009